SUPER DOOPER JEZEBEL

Tony Ross

Andersen Press · London

For Jan and Paul

An animated version of this book, together with four other stories by Tony Ross, is available from Tempo Video.

British Library Cataloguing in Publication Data
Ross, Tony
  Super dooper Jezebel.
  I. Title
  823'.914[J]   PZ7

  ISBN 0-86264-221-3

This book has been printed on 100% acid-free paper.

© 1988 by Tony Ross
First published in Great Britain by Andersen Press Ltd., 20 Vauxhall Bridge Road,
London SW1V 2SA. Published in Australia by Random Century Australia Pty., Ltd., 20 Alfred Street,
Milsons Point, Sydney, NSW 2061. All rights reserved. Colour separated in Switzerland
by Photolitho AG, Gossau, Zürich. Printed and bound in Italy by Grafiche AZ, Verona.
10 9 8 7 6 5 4

Jezebel was perfect in every way. She was so perfect,
she was called Super Dooper Jezebel.

When other children came out of school, they were
sometimes untidy,

but Jezebel was always super dooper neat.

Jezebel always kept her room tidy, and she always put her things back in their boxes . . .

and she cleaned up after the cat.

When she went out to play with her friends,

Jezebel always kept clean. (She still liked to have two baths every day).

She always wrote her "thank you" letters, in neat
writing, without being reminded,

and at school, she was best at everything.

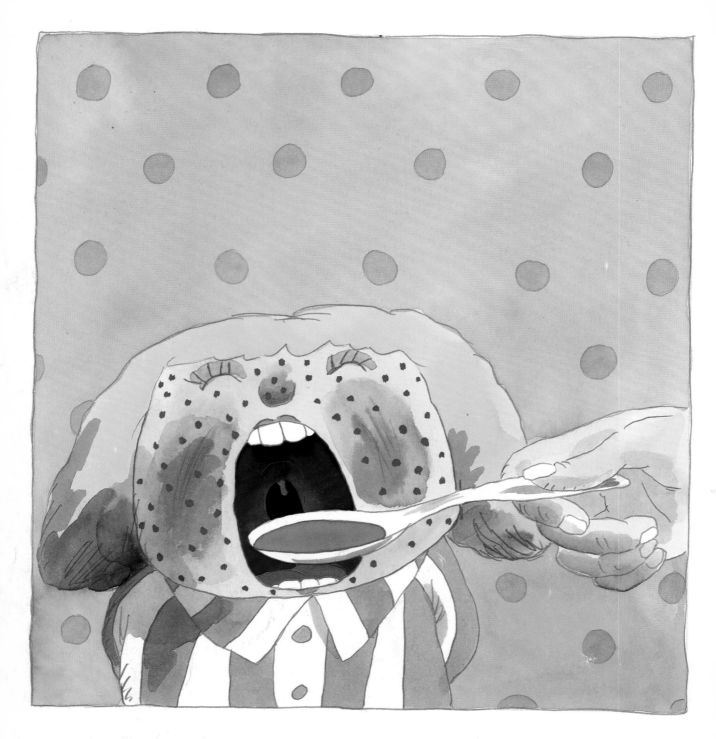

When she had spots, she always took her medicine
(and said, ''Thank you.'')

She could do up buttons, and tie real bows on her lace-ups.

Jezebel always ate up her meals. She always put
her knife and fork together,

and she *never* picked her nose.

Jezebel told other children not to do things . . .

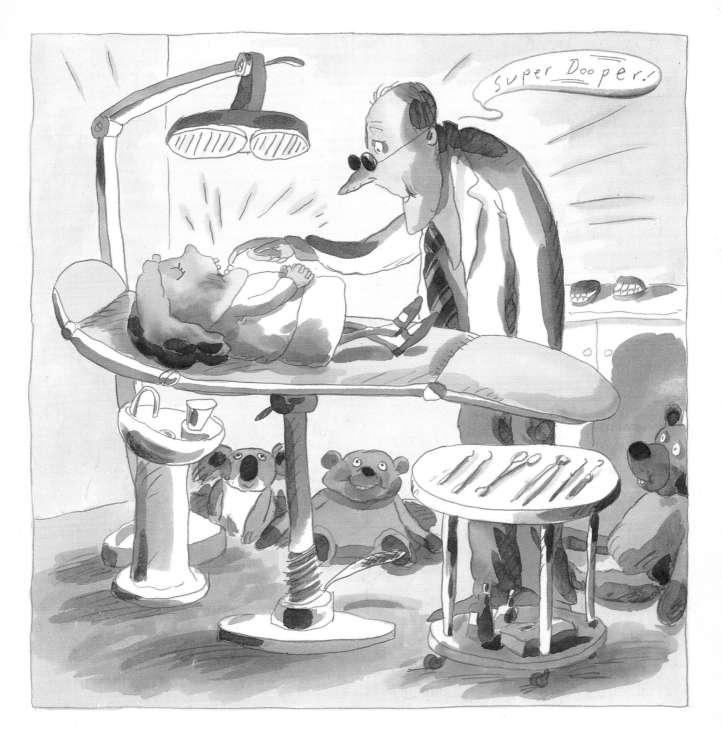

because it was nice being perfect.

When the Prime Minister heard about Jezebel,
she sent a special medal for being good,

and a special statue of Jezebel was put up in the park, to remind everybody else to try to be perfect.

She even went on television, in a special show
to talk about herself and her medal,

and the cups she had won for being polite, being spotless, being helpful, being best at sums, reading, poetry and writing.

At school, Super Dooper Jezebel wouldn't do *anything* wrong . . .

like the other noisy children who weren't perfect . . .

CLUMP!

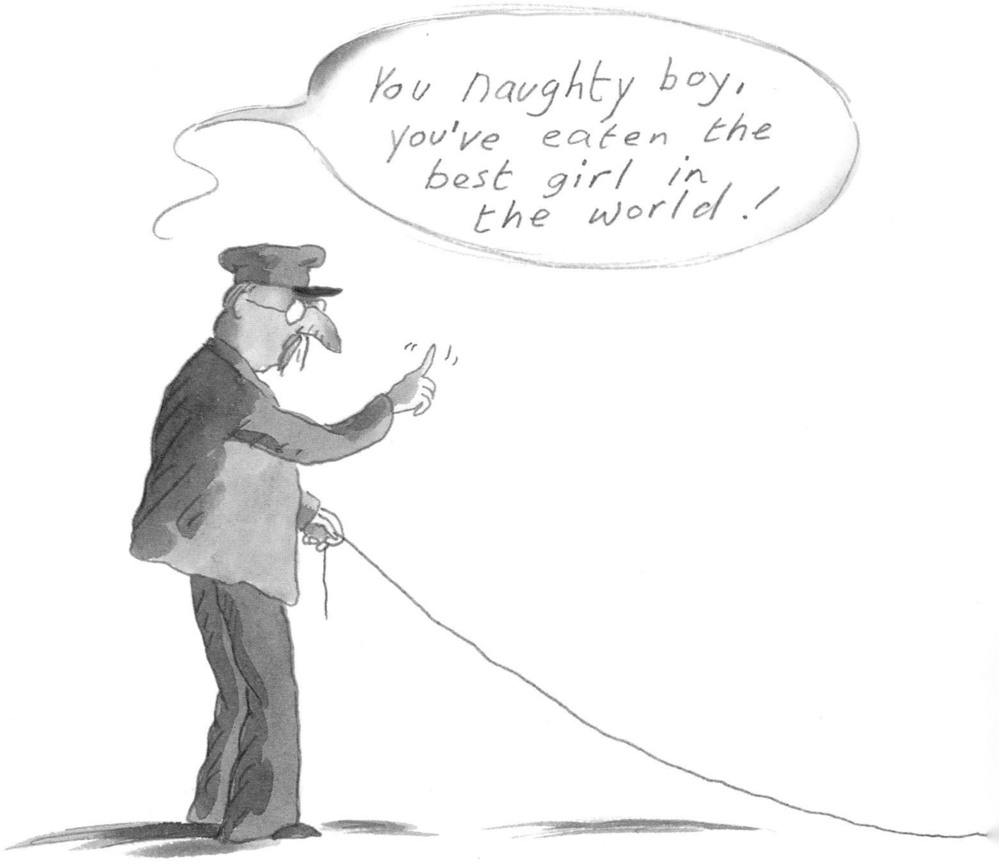
You naughty boy, you've eaten the best girl in the world!